THIS is NOT a Fairy Tale

BY WILL MABBITT

& FRED BLUNT

PUFFIN

It was almost time for tea . . .

Dad opened the book and began to read . . .

Once upon a time there was a princess . . .

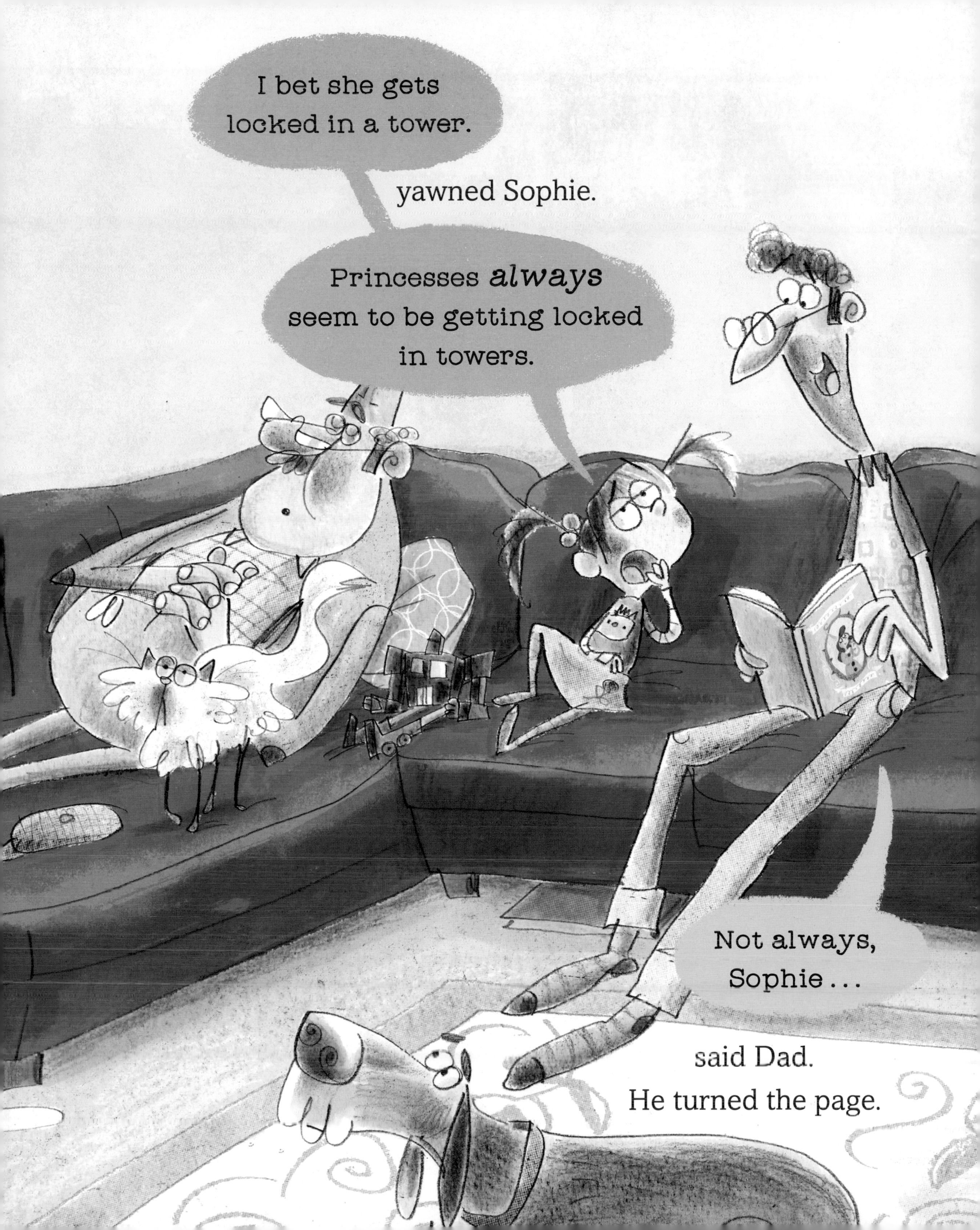

yawned Sophie.

said Dad.
He turned the page.

One day a prince was riding through the kingdom.

The prince *always* gets to ride the horse. The princess never gets to have a go.

said Sophie.

Maybe this princess doesn't have her own horse.

said Dad.

Yes...

agreed Sophie.

That's why she'll have to borrow one!
She'll need to borrow some armour too.

THE PRINCE!

puff

The princess rode across the kingdom

ZZZZZZZZZ

in search of the tower.

I think towers
are usually hidden in
a forest of thorns.

said Sophie.

Not always,
Sophie...

said Dad.

...a COMBINE HARVESTER would be much quicker!

I'm not sure that's going to work. **The prince is BALD!** I've got a better idea...

ACTIVATE
TRANSFORMATION!

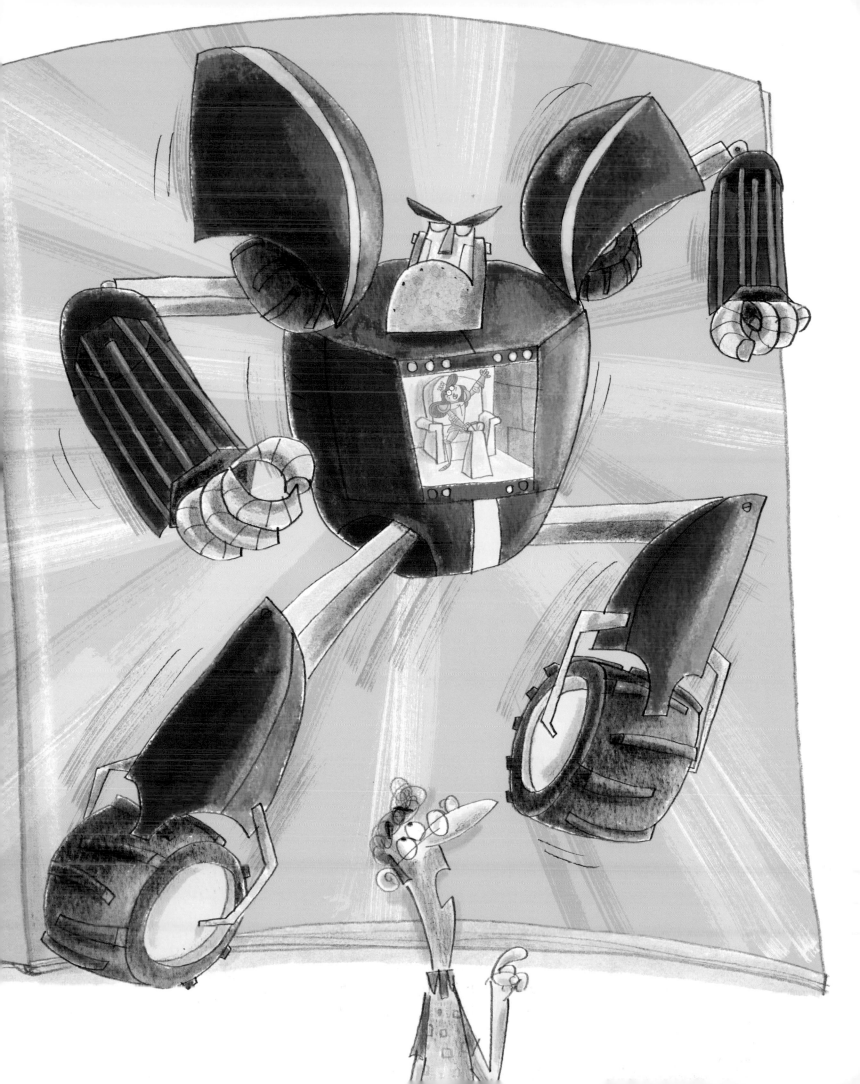

Rescue mission
ACCOMPLISHED . . .

The princess
is under attack!

said Sophie.

WAIT!
OOOF
AAAA AAAA AA
Thud
There's something WRONG with the dragon.

said Sophie.

AAAA
LOOK! He's got a poorly bottom. He's sat on something pointy.
No wonder he's so upset!

AHHHHH

HOORAY
for the princess!

shouted Dad.

Dad turned over to the last page.

The princess and her friends celebrated with a feast...

And they ALL lived...

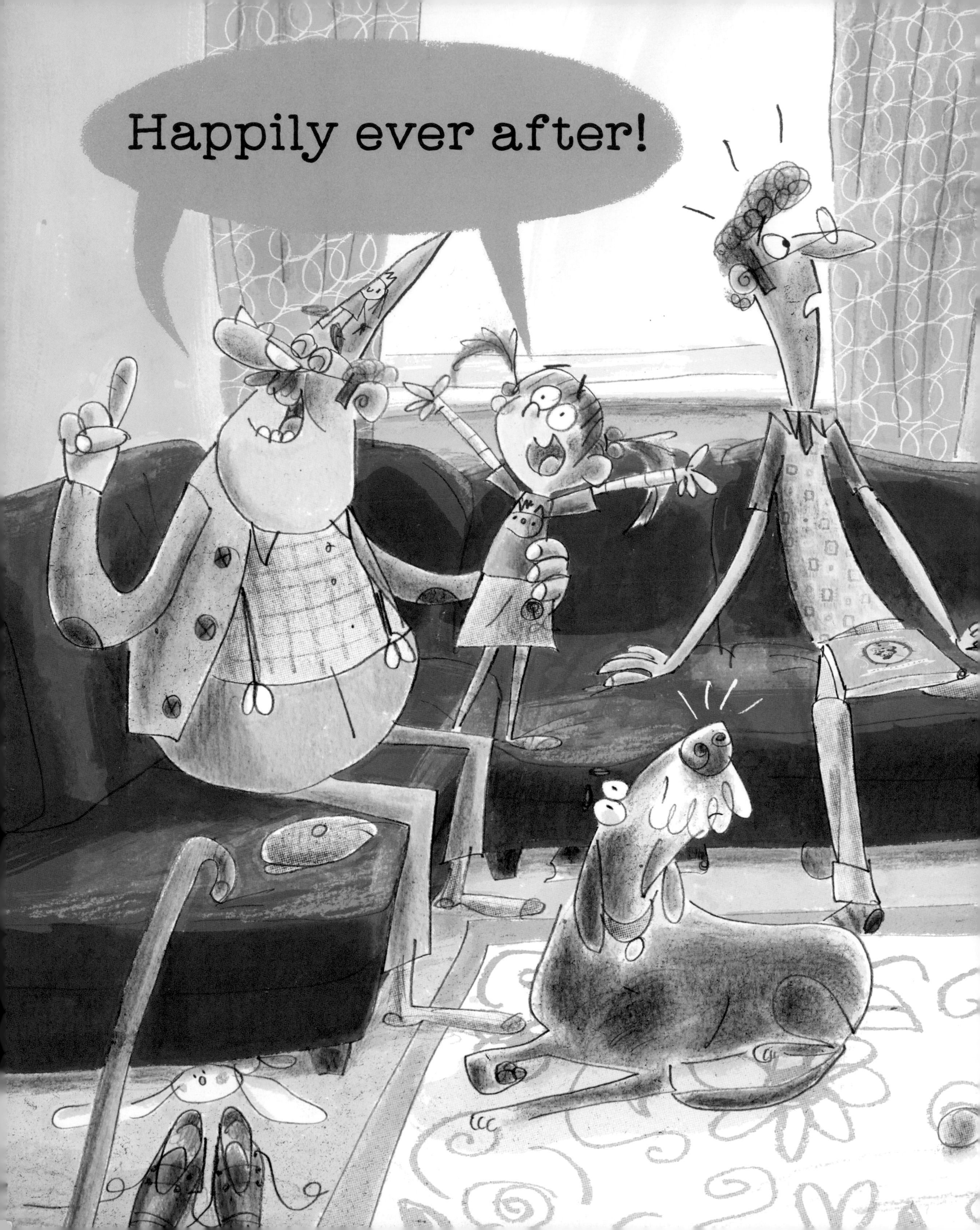
Happily ever after!

For Berta whose dad burns sausages too – W. M.

For Bonnie and Sonny – F. B.

PUFFIN BOOKS
UK | USA | Canada | Ireland | Australia | India | New Zealand | South Africa
Puffin Books is part of the Penguin Random House group of companies
whose addresses can be found at global.penguinrandomhouse.com.
www.penguin.co.uk   www.puffin.co.uk   www.ladybird.co.uk

 Penguin
Random House
UK

First published 2017
001
Text copyright © Will Mabbitt, 2017
Illustrations copyright © Fred Blunt, 2017
The moral right of the author and illustrator has been asserted
Made and printed in China
A CIP catalogue record for this book is available from the British Library
ISBN: 978–0–141–36882–5